YOU ARE NEW

FOR BOOPS—L. K.

Library of Congress Cataloging-in-Publication Data:

Names: Knisley, Lucy, author, illustrator.
Title: You are new / by Lucy Knisley.
Description: San Francisco, California : Chronicle Books LLC, [2019] |
    Summary: When you are a brand-new baby there are many things you can do in
    the world—and when you get bigger there are even more new experiences.
Identifiers: LCCN 2017061557 | ISBN 9781452161563 (alk. paper)
Subjects: LCSH: Infants—Juvenile fiction. | Experience in children—Juvenile
    fiction. | Growth—Juvenile fiction. | CYAC: Stories in rhyme. |
    Babies—Fiction. | Growth—Fiction.
Classification: LCC PZ8.3.K749 Yo 2019 | DDC [E]—dc23 LC record available
at https://lccn.loc.gov/2017061557

Manufactured in China.

Design by Lucy Knisley and Jennifer Tolo Pierce.
Typeset in Dolly.
The illustrations in this book were rendered using digital collage.

10 9 8 7 6 5 4 3 2 1

Chronicle books and gifts are available at special quantity discounts to
corporations, professional associations, literacy programs, and other
organizations. For details and discount information, please contact our
premiums department at corporatesales@chroniclebooks.com or at
1-800-759-0190.

Chronicle Books LLC
680 Second Street
San Francisco, California 94107

Chronicle Books—we see things differently. Become part of
our community at www.chroniclekids.com.

YOU ARE NEW

BY LUCY KNISLEY

chronicle books·san francisco

HELLO, YOU!

YOU ARE NEW.

WHEN YOU'RE NEW . . .

WHAT CAN YOU DO?

YOU CAN
LOOK AND SEE AND PEER.

YOU
CAN
TOUCH
AND
TASTE
AND
HEAR.

YOU CAN DOZE

AND

NAP

AND

SNOOZE.

IT MAKES YOU SLEEPY, BEING NEW.

YOU CAN FIT
IN TINY SPOTS.

YOU GET CARRIED QUITE A LOT!

YOU WEAR LITTLE BABY SHOES.

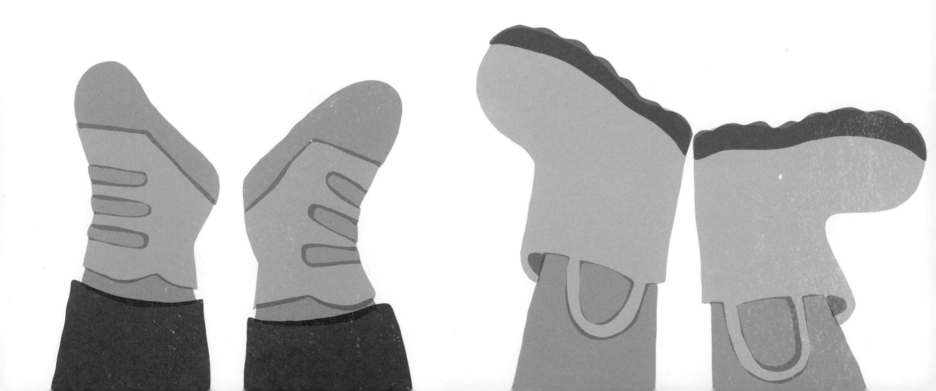

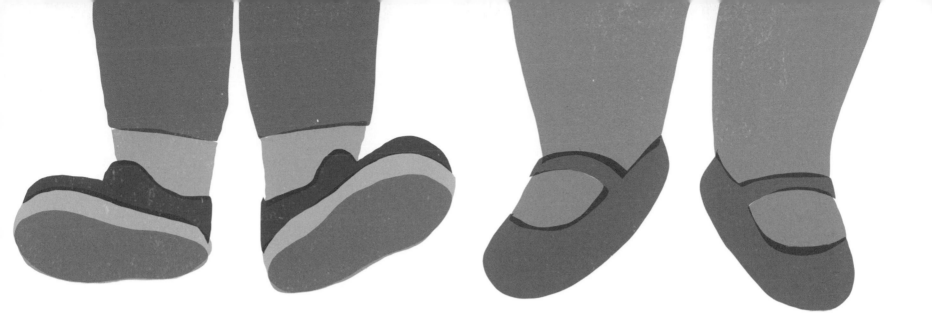

IT'S VERY CUTE
WHEN YOU ARE NEW.

YOU CAN OPEN WIDE AND YELL.

YOU GET MAD AND SCARED AND BLUE.

IT'S TOUGH WHEN EVERYTHING IS NEW.

YOU TAKE
BATHS,

WASH OFF
THE GRIME,

THEN GET
CUDDLED.

COZY TIME!

YOU PLAY
GAMES,
LIKE . . .

PEEKABOO!

IT'S PRETTY
AWESOME
BEING NEW.

EVERY DAY YOU STRETCH AND GROW.

YOU LEARN
SOMETHING . . .

THEN
YOU
KNOW.

LOOK AT YOU,
YOU'VE GROWN SO TALL.

SOON YOU WON'T BE
NEW AT ALL.

BUT WAIT!

YOU WILL BE NEW AGAIN.

YOU'LL LEARN NEW GAMES.

YOU'LL MAKE
NEW FRIENDS.

A BRAND-NEW BOOK
UPON THE SHELF—

A WHOLE NEW WAY TO SEE YOURSELF.

NEW WORLDS, NEW PLACES, NEW ADVENTURES...

MEETING YOUR NEW FAMILY MEMBER.

YOU'LL TRY NEW THINGS.

YOU'LL MEET NEW FOLKS.

YOU'LL PICK NEW FAVORITES . . .

HEAR NEW JOKES.

YOU MIGHT NOT KNOW JUST WHAT TO DO . . .

THAT'S OKAY
WHEN YOU
ARE NEW.

A WORLD OF BEING NEW IS WAITING—

EXCITING . . . COOL . . .

AND FASCINATING.

AND WHEN
YOU LOVE . . .

AND YOU'RE LOVED, TOO . . .

JUST LIKE THAT, YOU ARE NEW.